Art and Anger

PRAISE FOR *STORYSHARES*

"One of the brightest innovators and game-changers in the education industry."
– Forbes

"Your success in applying research-validated practices to promote literacy serves as a valuable model for other organizations seeking to create evidence-based literacy programs."
- Library of Congress

"We need powerful social and educational innovation, and Storyshares is breaking new ground. The organization addresses critical problems facing our students and teachers. I am excited about the strategies it brings to the collective work of making sure every student has an equal chance in life."
– Teach For America

"Around the world, this is one of the up-and-coming trailblazers changing the landscape of literacy and education."
- International Literacy Association

"It's the perfect idea. There's really nothing like this. I mean wow, this will be a wonderful experience for young people."   - Andrea Davis Pinkney, Executive Director, Scholastic

"Reading for meaning opens opportunities for a lifetime of learning. Providing emerging readers with engaging texts that are designed to offer both challenges and support for each individual will improve their lives for years to come. Storyshares is a wonderful start."
- David Rose, Co-founder of CAST & UDL

Art and Anger

Nolan Janssens

STORYSHARES

Story Share, Inc.
New York. Boston. Philadelphia

Copyright © 2022 by Nolan Janssens

All rights reserved.

Published in the United States by Story Share, Inc.

The characters and events in this book are fictitious. Any similarity to real persons, living or dead, is entirely coincidental.

Storyshares
Story Share, Inc.
24 N. Bryn Mawr Avenue #340
Bryn Mawr, PA 19010-3304
www.storyshares.org

Inspiring reading with a new kind of book.

Interest Level: High School
Grade Level Equivalent: 1.3

9781642614657

Book design by Storyshares

Printed in the United States of America

Storyshares Presents

1

Everyone in my class stares at me and whispers. They're all wondering if the rumors are true. Am I really as bad as they say? Maybe I am.

The teacher doesn't seem to notice that all the students are pointing at me. It's possible that she also thinks I'm a psycho. All I want is for this class to end so that I can find some people who have never heard of me before.

Eleven o'clock. Ten past eleven. Fifteen past eleven. And finally, twenty past eleven. It's time for lunch.

It takes me fifteen minutes — longer than it should — to find the cafeteria. My old school had half the number of hallways. I'm too distracted by all the new faces to keep track of where I'm going.

When I finally arrive at the cafeteria, I realize that I'm probably the only student who enrolled halfway through the school year. That means that every group has already claimed a specific table. Now I have to decide who seems least likely to reject me.

I notice a group of people sitting at one of the tables. They look like they're in grade ten or eleven. I know that they are a grade or two higher than me. Maybe that means they won't know the rumors.

"Hi," I manage to say, in a voice higher than I intended.

They all grab their cell phones and act too busy to hear me.

"Can I sit here?" I ask.

Nobody answers. I decide to sit at the edge of the table. Everyone stands up and leaves the second I sit down.

I can see and smell many different types of food. I smell curry spices, fish, and some aromas that I don't know. I see steaming noodles, burritos, and some strange blubbery looking things. I even see people sharing Roquefort cheese and a baguette. Last year, when I lived in a small town called Lumby, kids would have called me a fart-eater for eating something like that.

The smelly cheese reminds me of the food I ate as a little kid in Belgium. I don't remember much of Belgium, but I don't think people hated me like they did in Lumby. My mom keeps telling me how diverse Vancouver is and that I won't get bullied.

Maybe she would have been right if it weren't for the rumors.

2

Finally, school is over for the day. All that's left is a twenty-minute bus ride to get home. I feel like I've been on the bus for ten minutes already. I check my cell phone. It's only been three minutes.

I grab my sharpie marker and start to draw giant robots on the ugly, brown seat in front of me. I'm not sure why. I just like robots, and I'm pretty sure they're going to take over the world one day.

My dad used to complain about that sort of thing. Technology. But I don't think robots would do a worse job of running the planet than humans.

"Hey, kid!" yells the bus driver. "What the heck do you think you're doing vandalizing my bus?"

Suddenly, the bus is quiet. Even the people at the back of the bus stop talking.

"Sorry."

"Is that all you can say? How much further do you live?" asks the bus driver.

"Not far," I lie.

"Lucky you. You're walking."

The bus driver pulls up at the next stop, and I get up to leave.

"What's your name?" he asks.

"Noah."

"I need your last name."

"Oh, uh..." I now realize that he wants to report me and that I should lie if I don't want to get into trouble. "Smith."

I figure that I should use a common last name.

"You can expect a phone call from your principal this week."

I can feel everyone staring at me as I exit the bus.

4

3

I have only been walking for ten minutes, and I have already seen over one hundred cars. In Lumby, I would have seen two farms and maybe a couple of cows.

One of the reasons my dad wanted to move to Lumby was because he hated traffic. He hated a lot of things, but he loved the nature and wilderness in Canada. As a photographer, he wanted to capture vast landscapes. He wanted to see a world untouched by people. And Lumby definitely didn't have a lot of people.

Especially foreign ones.

There's a lot less traffic once I leave the main road. Giant trees decorate both sides of the street, but it's January, and all the leaves have fallen off.

The houses in my neighborhood are high and narrow. A few of the homes are made from bricks, like in Belgium. Most of them look old and run-down, and I like those more than some of the modern houses.

"Hey!" I hear someone yell. "Come over here."

I look around and see a girl on a skateboard waving at me. She has long black hair, and she's wearing a black hoodie and ripped jeans. She hops off her skateboard, and suddenly I recognize her. She goes to my school. She must be in grade eleven or twelve.

"You're the new kid, right?" she says.

"Yeah," I answer.

"What's your name?"

"Noah."

"I'm Natasha. My friends call me Tash."

"Hi, Natasha."

"Call me Tash."

"Oh, okay," I say.

I look around to see if there's a group of people filming us. Maybe she's about to play a prank on me.

"Do you live close to here?" she asks.

"A few blocks further. Near Eighth Street."

"The bus drops you off there, you know."

"Yeah, I know."

"Did the bus driver kick you off the bus?"

"Well, I—"

"He kicked you off the bus," she says with a proud smile.

"How do you know?"

"Because he's a grumpy old man," says Tash. "Do you skateboard?"

"No."

"Want to?"

"Sure," I say, wondering why the heck this older girl wants to hang out with me.

"I have another skateboard. Follow me."

I hesitate for a second because I know my mom is expecting me to be home soon. I quickly text my mom and tell her that I'm going to be home later than expected.

4

We walk two blocks, and then Natasha points at her house. We walk up a creaking wooden staircase towards the front door.

The porch is full of hanging baskets and pots filled with various types of herbs. Some of the herbs are purple, some of them are green, and they all make the air smell spicy and sweet.

She rubs her fingers on a leaf without ripping it from the plant. The leaf is small and green, and the plant has many yellow flowers.

"Smell my fingers," Tash says.

She pushes her hand towards my face. At first, I don't smell anything because I'm too distracted by her touching my face. Then I notice that the scent is familiar.

"They smell like popcorn," I say.

"That's why they call it a popcorn plant. They're originally from central and eastern Africa."

"Oh cool," I say.

"Are you interested in botany?"

"What's that?"

"It's the study of plants."

"Oh yeah, I like plants," I say, realizing that I probably sound like an idiot.

"None of the girls in my grade talk about anything interesting. It's always boys and blah blah blah."

"That's too bad," I say, even though I really want to know what they say about boys.

She opens her front door. I follow her inside.

There's Native American art everywhere. There's a soapstone carving of a bear, a wooden mask that looks like an angry eagle, and paintings of mountains and rivers just like my dad used to photograph.

"Yo, Dad, we have a visitor," says Tash.

"Come into the kitchen," he shouts.

We walk into the kitchen, and I see a tall man with hair past his shoulder blades. He's cooking a giant pot of curry and drinking a glass of wine. He looks like he is First Nations, but he doesn't look like Tash.

"You're cooking dinner?" Tash asks.

"I'm following one of your mom's recipes."

"But she doesn't write down her curry recipes."

"I know. That's the problem," he says, and he and Tash laugh in a way that's almost identical.

"By the way, this is Noah," says Tash. "Noah, this is my dad, Ernie."

Ernie dries his hand off on a cloth and shakes my hand.

"Nice to meet you, Noah. Are you adjusting to the new city?" Ernie asks.

I wonder how he knows that I'm not from here. Do adults know the rumors about me, too?

"Oh yeah, I like it. I was close to a city when I lived in Belgium. I'm kind of used to it."

"You've traveled a lot, then, huh? What do your parents do?"

"My mom is working as a secretary right now. My dad used to be a professional photographer."

"What does he do now?" Ernie asks.

"He died last year."

"I'm sorry to hear that."

"Happens to everyone," I say, angrier than I intended. "Should we grab your other board and go shred now?"

I remember hearing skateboarders use the word shred.

"Yeah, sure," says Tash.

"Nice meeting you, Noah," Ernie says.

"You too."

14

5

I follow Tash to a small skateboard park several blocks away. All the concrete is covered in graffiti art. There are so many spray-painted words and paintings. Some are colorful and detailed, but others look like black scribbles.

I keep thinking that if I spray painted one of my robots, it would look pretty cool here.

The few people skateboarding perform all sorts of tricks that I don't think I could ever do.

"Check this out," Tash says.

She performs a trick called a kickflip. She jumps up with the board, the board flips entirely around in the air, and then she lands on it again.

She teaches me how to stand on my board and how to ride it on a flat surface. Without telling her, I take it down a small hill, hoping to impress her.

"You're a natural," Tash says.

I'm too concentrated to think about anything but keeping my balance. It feels good. I ride down a bigger ramp. Suddenly, the skateboard flies out from under me, and I fall flat on my back. It hurts like hell, but I don't want to let Tash know that.

"Dude, are you okay? Want to go home?" Tash asks.

"Naw, I'm good. I'll just sit it out for a bit," I tell her.

"Okay, is it cool if I rip around for a bit?"

"Yeah, for sure."

I watch her skateboard on all the park features. She's just as good as the other people here.

After several minutes, I hear a spraying sound behind me. I look back and see a group of people spray painting a ramp. Most of them look like they have graduated, but one of them looks like he might be Tash's age. He notices me staring. I quickly look away.

"What are you looking at, kid?" he asks.

"Your friend's graffiti," I manage to say. "It's pretty tight, man."

"Don't call me 'man.' I'm not your friend."

"Sorry," I mumble.

"Wait, I know you. Aren't you the new freak?"

Oh, no. I grab my skateboard and start to walk away.

"Don't you know it's rude to walk away when someone asks you a question?"

I can hear him following me, but I decide not to make eye contact.

"Hey!" he yells, and then shoves me to the ground. I fall and hit my forehead on a metal rail.

"Leave me alone," I say as I get up.

"You're a psycho. A little, small-town psycho," he says, but I keep ignoring him. "Is your mom crazy? 'Cause I like crazy ladies."

"Shut up!" I yell.

"What's going on here, guys?" Tash says as she skateboards over.

I look around, and everyone else is gathering around us.

"What about your dad? I bet he's a psycho, too," the older boy says.

I can't take it anymore. I grab my skateboard and swing it as hard as I can at one of his legs. He grabs his leg in pain, and I push him to the ground. For a second I think about how much bigger and older he is than me, but as quickly as the thought comes into my mind, it leaves. I jump on him, and before I can punch him, I feel Tash and someone else dragging me away.

"Noah, stop it!" Tash screams as I try to wiggle free.

"What are you doing with this freak?" says the boy as a guy with tattooed arms and an older girl lift him up from the ground.

"Ethan, just screw off, okay?" Tash says.

Oh great, they know each other.

Ethan tries to come toward me, but the older girl whispers something in his ear and he stops.

"You're lucky everyone here is Tash's friend, freak. You better hope I never see you alone."

"Well, he'll definitely never see you at school," says Tash.

"Don't worry, you'll get to lay your eyes on me in class one day again. I haven't dropped out yet, babe."

"Gross," says Tash as she grabs me by the arm. "Let's get out of here."

We skateboard the whole way home. Tash doesn't say a word to me.

You can't control what happens to you, only how you choose to react. I keep thinking about all the things my anger management counselor used to tell me. Nothing seems to work.

"My place is just around the corner," I say.

"Okay, cool. Meet me in the student parking at lunch tomorrow," says Tash.

"For sure," I say, trying not to sound too excited.

"And no hitting people with skateboards, Noah," she says and then laughs.

I can tell her laugh is forced.

6

My mom takes dinner out of the oven the second I walk inside. She made Belgian endives wrapped in ham with cheese sauce, a meal that I haven't eaten in many years. Endives are more bitter than most vegetables, but when they're covered in melted cheese and ham, I love them.

At first, my mom can't stop talking about how many more grocery options there are in Vancouver than in Lumby. Whenever she talks about food, she speaks in

Flemish and sometimes in French — the languages that she grew up with. She says it's because when talking about food in those languages, she can almost taste what she's talking about.

I never understood that.

When she finally sits down at the table, she looks at me and asks about the bruise on my forehead. I tried to cover it with my hair, but it's not long enough.

"I fell skateboarding," I say.

"I'll grab you an icepack."

I try to tell her that I'm fine. Before I can say anything, she stands up and hurries to the kitchen. I can hear her say a couple of Flemish swearwords. She returns with a bottle of beer.

"I forgot to buy ice packs. This should help," my mom says as she holds the cold bottle of beer to my forehead.

"Mama, can you please sit down? I'm okay," I tell her.

"Okay, okay," she says.

We talk about Tash a bit. I try to avoid questions about school. When it's finally time to do the dishes, I tell her that I have homework to do.

"Let me know if you need any help," she says.

"It's math."

Suddenly her smile disappears. She quickly finishes her glass of wine and starts to do the dishes.

I shouldn't have said anything.

My dad always helped me with math.

Art and Anger

7

Today, we're learning about the Industrial Revolution. The social studies teacher, Miss Jacobs, tells us that revolutions change the world and our lives.

I'm not too sure things really change. There is always someone getting hurt and someone else doing the hurting.

Miss Jacobs wants us to make a list of all the technologies we use in our daily lives. She also wants us to guess which technologies were invented during the industrial age. She tells us to choose groups of three or four to discuss our lists.

Five minutes later, I'm stuck without a group.

"Does anyone have room for Noah in their group?" Miss Jacobs asks.

None of my classmates offer to let me join their group.

Miss Jacobs puts me in a group with two girls. They tell me that they moved here from China a few months ago. Both of them are kind to me. I assume they don't know the rumors. We don't end up having much of a discussion though; we just quietly add to our lists.

After several minutes, Miss Jacobs asks what we wrote down. Every group mentions cell phones, computers, and some sort of social media. Most people don't mention any inventions from the industrial age.

Miss Jacobs tells us about the start of factories, the typewriter, the tin can, telegraph communication, and the first modern battery. She explains that many of the things we enjoy today would not have been possible without the Industrial Revolution. She also explains some of the horrible working standards and child labor that occurred before the Industrial Revolution.

"They should put weirdos like that new kid to work in factories," I hear a boy whisper at the table behind me.
Everyone snickers and whispers some things that I can't hear.

Miss Jacobs tells the table to be quiet. She tries to start a class discussion about what we consider the most critical invention from the industrial age.

One guy shouts out, "the tin can," but I zone out for the rest of the conversation. I just want it to be lunchtime already.

Eleven o'clock. Ten past eleven. Fifteen past eleven. And finally, twenty past eleven. It's time for lunch.

I go to the student parking lot right away. I sit on the curb, waiting for Tash and her friends. After twenty minutes I start to tell myself they aren't going to show up. Suddenly, an old, dark green SUV drives into the parking lot at full speed. Whoever is driving slams on the brakes.

"Yo, Noah!" Tash shouts from the passenger window.
Tash and two guys jump out from the vehicle.

"Sorry we're late. We went to grab some burgers. I got you a milkshake," Tash says.

"Oh, thanks."

"This is Jason," says Tash, pointing to a guy wearing a trucker hat backwards.

"'Sup," Jason says as he sticks out his fist for a pound.

The other guy grabs four skateboards from the trunk and hands out one to each of us. He looks like the type of guy who never stops smiling.

"And this is Matty."

"A new little shredder! What's up?" says Matt, and then he grabs my hand and pulls me in for a hug.

"I'm not any good yet," I say.

"Screw it," says Matt. "That's why we practice."

"We gotta go across the street, though. We're not allowed to skateboard here," says Tash.

I'm just about to hop on my skateboard when I hear, "Noah Martens, please report to the principal's office. Noah Martens, please report to the principal's office," on the PA system.

"Did you hear that?" I ask.

"I think so. It's kind of hard to hear the announcements outside," Tash says.

"Yo, you two coming or what?" Matt asks, already on his skateboard.

"I think we heard Noah's name get called. I'm going with him," Tash says.

"We'll catch you later, then," Matt says.

Tash and I walk into the school office. The receptionist says that the principal will be with me shortly.

"Hi, Noah," says Principal Raza.

I know her from when I had my orientation.

"Hi, Principal Raza," I say.

"Hi, Mom," says Tash. "What did Noah do?"

Did she just say "Mom?"

"That's none of your business, Natasha. I need to talk to Noah alone."

"Fine. I'll see you later, Noah."

Principal Raza takes me into her office. First, she asks me how I'm doing and if I'm adjusting to the new school.

I tell her that Tash has been kind to me and that I enjoy what I'm learning. I don't tell her about all the whispers and how people avoid me.

She already knows about the rumors. She knows the truth.

"And do you know why I called you to the office today, Noah?" Principal Raza asks.

"No."

"Are you sure? It's better if you tell me."

"Well, what's it about?" I ask.

"The bus," she says.

"Oh... I told the driver I was sorry. I don't know why I drew those pictures."

"Adjusting to a new school can be difficult, Noah. Maybe you're angry at someone or something, but vandalizing and damaging school property is not the answer," she says.

"I'm sorry," I say.

"I'm only giving you an in-school suspension for one week. That includes next week, Monday and Tuesday."

"What does that mean?" I ask.

"You have garbage duty every day at lunchtime and recess."

"I see. Can I go now, Principal Raza?"

"Yes, you may. And next time, draw on something that belongs to you."

"Okay, thank you," I say as I stand up to leave.

"And I'm happy that you're making friends. Tash is a good kid, but watch out for some of her friends, Noah."

I nod and leave. "Watch out for Ethan" is what she should have said.

32

8

Tash approaches me at the bus loading zone after school.

"What happened?" Tash asks.

"I got in trouble for drawing on one of the bus seats," I say.

"I hope my mom wasn't too hard on you."

"I don't think so. I got an in-school suspension for a week."

Art and Anger

"Well, this might cheer you up." Tash opens her bag. There are four cans of spray paint in it.

"You seemed to be into the graffiti yesterday. I know of an old house that we could spray paint."

"I probably shouldn't risk it," I say.

"Naw, it's all good. My dad knows the owner. The house is getting torn down next month," Tash says.

"So would our painting, then."

"Art should reflect life, right?" Tash points out.

"I guess so," I say.

"Then it needs to come to an end one day. The memory can live on."

"When do you wanna go?" I ask, not sure what else to say.

"Now. The place is on our way home. We can just take the bus."

I notice a group of boys and girls staring at us. They look confused. Probably because I'm hanging out with a grade twelve girl. Tash doesn't seem to notice though. Maybe she just doesn't care.

The bus arrives after a few minutes. The bus driver glares at me when I walk inside.

"Next time you should use a better alias," he says.

"Okay, sorry," I say to the bus driver. "What's an alias?" I ask Tash.

"It's a fake name."

"Oh, that makes sense."

Tash laughs and then asks, "What name did you use?"

"Noah Smith. I thought of using a fake name after I said my first name."

Tash bursts out laughing. Her whole body shakes when she laughs.

I want to tell her that she's beautiful. Maybe I should say "hot." That's what most guys say. Either way, I probably shouldn't say anything. She might feel weirded out.

The bus arrives at our stop. I look back and notice that almost everyone is staring at us. Once Tash steps off the bus, I hear a girl say, "I bet she feels bad for that freak."

Tash wraps her arm around my shoulder as we walk down the sidewalk. I put my arm around her shoulder. I have to reach up because she's taller than me. We walk all the way to the run-down old house like that.

"All right, so I think we should go inside through that broken window. If we paint inside, we won't be bothered by anyone," Tash says.

"Works for me. What do you want to paint?"

"Something that makes me feel things I can't understand. What about you?"

"Um, robots."

Tash laughs and then says, "I can work with that. I'll start over on this side of the wall, and you start over on that side. We should come here every day after school. Make a damn masterpiece."

"I'm down," I say.

I start by painting the outline of two robots. I decide that they should be holding something. I just don't know what yet. I look over at Tash. We've only been painting for fifteen minutes, and she has already used four different colors. I don't think she likes outlines.

My phone rings.

"Hi, Mom," I say.

"Get over here right now, Noah. I heard that you've been vandalizing school property."

I tell her that I've already received my punishment and that Principal Raza didn't seem too mad. It's no use, though. I have to go home right away.

"Let's see who's a faster runner," says Tash.

"What?"

"The last one to your place has to buy the winner a pizza tomorrow!"

We run all the way to my place. It's at least fifteen blocks away. We scream, "On your left!" when we pass a group of middle-aged women walking with hiking poles. I think one of them shouts, but I'm running too hard to know for sure.

One more block!

Tash beats me, just barely. We collapse on the ground, panting.

"Make sure that your mom calls mine. I can't let your mom ground you. We have a mural to finish," Tash says.

"Will do."

"See ya tomorrow," Tash says as she stands up to leave.

"See ya!" I say.

I slowly open the door to my home and find my mom waiting for me in the kitchen. I can tell that she's already had a few glasses of wine. My mom repeats everything that she said on the phone. She's more emotional than she should be. She wants me to come home right after school for the rest of the month.

I tell her that I have an art project to do with the principal's daughter after school every day. We argue for several more minutes. My father would have called it negotiating. She decides that my curfew will be five o'clock in the evening for three weeks.

My father said there were no winners and losers in negotiations, but I think that's because he wasn't very good at it.

40

9

Class, garbage duty, class, garbage duty, class, garbage duty, class, paint, and repeat. The people in my class keep avoiding me. The teachers keep teaching. Garbage duty keeps sucking. However, I always have something to look forward to: Tash and our mural.

Finally, it's Friday. Tash and I hurry to our mural after school. I think we're almost halfway done. She has surrounded the painting of my robots with her many colors.

She tells me that my robots represent structure and an ugly future. Her colors represent chaos and beauty. I agree with her about the colors, but I don't know about the robots. I haven't decided what they should be holding yet. Tash wants me to choose.

I can't concentrate at all today.

Tash's torn clothes are covered in paint. Her hair looks more wild than usual. She seems so concentrated on our painting. It's as though the whole world could be on fire and she wouldn't know.

"I almost blinded a kid," I blurt out without really knowing why. After I moment I say, "I remember kids screaming. They were telling me to stop. I didn't stop. I couldn't stop. It was like time didn't exist."

The way Tash looks at me makes me want to tell her everything.

"I don't even know if I'm sorry for what I did. I think that's what made everything worse. The counselor and principal at my old school made me feel like I didn't care about anybody. But I really cared. I wanted everyone to like me. Nobody did."

"When I first moved to Canada, the kids made fun of my clothes, my food, my accent. They made fun of the sports I liked, the music I liked, and everything that I thought made me who I was," I say.

Tash keeps staring at me. It's like she understands everything that I'm saying, and it makes me want to cry. I hold back my tears, and my throat starts to hurt. Tash doesn't say a word.

"We had a drawing assignment one day. We had to make a self portrait. I couldn't stop thinking about my dad that month. I remember that he loved the drawings of the naked people that we saw in museums. I started to draw myself naked without even thinking about it."

"The boy I ended up beating up, Travis, grabbed my drawing and held it up in front of the whole class. Everyone laughed or called me a pervert. The teacher looked disgusted and sent me to the principal's office. I only received a warning, probably because the principal knew that my Dad passed away a month before."

"I think my mom would have defended me, but I didn't tell her," I continue. "She had enough to worry about. Instead, I just got angrier. Nothing was fair."

"Then one day, out of nowhere, Travis apologized and asked me to skip school with him and his friends from another school. I was so excited that I didn't care about the drawing incident anymore. The next day, we ended up going to the beach, and Travis dared me to go skinny dipping. I had to swim to the buoy and back. Once I got to the buoy, I saw them all running away with my clothes and backpack."

"As I was walking to school, a police officer saw me. He gave me a blanket and brought me back to school. I explained everything to the principal, but Travis and his friends had the perfect plan. Travis had faked being sick. He made it home before his parents could tell he'd been gone. The kids from the other school had parents who worked graveyard shifts, so they didn't wake up till after the kids were back. All the parents confirmed that their kids were home. Worst of all, my clothes were in my cubby. I still don't know how that happened. I guess Travis gave my clothes to a friend at recess."

"I ended up getting a one-day suspension for streaking and skipping school. When I came back to school, all the kids made fun of me, which I expected. Then Travis walked in, and the teacher said that she hoped Travis felt better. Then Travis walked up to me and whispered that he actually was sick, but not as sick as my dad was. That's when I lost it. When the teacher tried to stop me, I hit her too. That's how I got expelled."

I look at Tash, and I can see tears in her eyes, but she looks frustrated.

After a moment, Tash says, "You're not the only who's been bullied. You can't even understand the things I have to go through."

"What do you mean?" I ask.

"Have you seen my parents? My mom is Indian. And by Indian I mean that she's from India. And my dad is First Nations. You know what means?"

"Well—"

"It means that I know how horrible people can be," Tash says, cutting me off. "Almost every time I travel, I get randomly checked by security. If I don't get randomly checked, it's usually my mom that does. And she doesn't seem to care because it doesn't compare to the racism she experienced as a kid."

"Then there's my dad. I know I look nothing like him, because most people have no idea that I'm First Nations. I get to hear all the things some people would never say in front of my dad's face. I call them the hidden racists, and there's a lot of them. You have no idea how many people look at us like we're drunks and losers," she says

"Well, they're all idiots," I say, unsure whether or not Tash is angry at me.

"Your school experience sounds horrible. I feel bad for you, but it's just high school. I'm going to have to deal with racism for the rest of my life. I know what happened to my grandparents. They got beaten and raped and had everything done to them to make them hate themselves. Those stories haunt me. They will always haunt me."

"That's beyond horrible, Tash," I say.

"People forget high school rumors," Tash says.

"Okay," I say, feeling confused. I thought Tash felt bad for me. Now it seems like she doesn't think I deserve to be angry or sad.

"Maybe we should get going. Isn't it almost your curfew?" Tash asks.

"Yeah, I guess so," I say.

We walk home in silence. I think about all the horrible things that have happened to people. Things that I will never fully relate to. I know that I'm better off than many people, but that doesn't make me feel better. Just because I know that other people experience pain doesn't mean that I don't still feel pain.

I want to tell Tash all of this, but I don't want to argue with her or make her more upset. I don't want to lose my only friend.

48

10

There's more garbage than usual today. Usually, I just pick up half-eaten sandwiches, plastic wrappings, and crunched-up homework. Now, I'm picking up beer cans and cigarette butts. I'm guessing that people party here on the weekends. I don't mind the work, though. It gives me time to think about the mural.

"'Sup, loser?" I hear someone say behind me.

I'm shoved to the ground before I can tell who it is. I turn around and see Ethan with his fists clenched.

"Stand up," he says.

I stand up. I'm confused by the smile on Ethan's face.

Suddenly, he punches me in the stomach. I heave for air while I listen to him laugh.

"I don't want to fight," I tell him.

He kicks me in the shin. I grab my leg, and he pushes me to the ground. Now, I just feel pain.

"You think you can embarrass me in front of my friends?" Ethan asks as he punches me again.

I escape from under him and try to pin him to the ground so that he can't hit me anymore. He knees me in the stomach and rolls on top of me.

"Noah!" Tash screams from a distance.

I hear her and some other people running toward me. Ethan tries to punch me. I cover my face, expecting a blow to the arms.

Suddenly, I feel his body lifted off of me. I look up and see Matty and Jason dragging Ethan away.

"Why are you guys protecting this freak?" Ethan asks.

"He's Tash's buddy, so now he's our buddy," Matty says.

"Tash's buddy," Ethan says. "Are you serious? She's the reason everyone hates him."

"Shut up, Ethan! Just shut up!" Tash screams.

I've never heard her scream before.

Ethan looks directly at me and says, "Do you know why everyone knows that you're a perverted psycho?"

"Stop it, Ethan," Tash says.

Matty is about to hit Ethan, but Jason holds him back.

"Tash is the one who told everyone about you. The naked freak," Ethan says.

"What's he talking about, Tash?" I ask.

"Noah, please. Just ignore him," Tash says.

"How have you not figured it out? Everyone knew the rumors before you got here. Obviously, it's the principal's daughter. She overheard her mom and told everyone," Ethan says.

"Why did you do that?" I ask.

"I didn't tell everyone, Noah," Tash says. "I told a few people, and the rumors spread. I'm sorry."

She's just like everyone else.

I don't even want to respond. I'm afraid that if I say something, I'll cry.

I run away.

Tash runs after me, telling me that's she's sorry.

"Screw off!" I scream.

She stops. I keep running. I'm not sure where I'm going. I just know that I don't want to be here. I don't want to be anywhere.

11

I arrive at the mural. It feels like my feet carried me here without my control.

I think about all the time that Tash and I spent here. Was she only hanging out with me because she felt bad for what she had done?

I look around and notice how much junk is in this old house. I guess I got used to spotting out the garbage. Pop cans, torn-up garbage bags, rusted buckets of paint...

Suddenly, I notice an old staple gun.

I begin stapling everything I can find to the mural. Pop cans, bags of chips, and I even see a pair of dirty, old pants. I notice how many brand logos there are on the garbage. I only cover my robots' feet with garbage, plus some of the background: Tash's chaos of colors.

I want to cover everything she painted.

I suddenly feel exhausted. I lie on the ground, close my eyes, and wait for my thoughts to disappear.

When I open my eyes, it's almost dark out. I realize that I must have fallen asleep. I thought that I was dreaming about my mom's voice, but then I hear it loud and clear.

"Noah, are you here?" my mom calls.

Before I can say another word, my mom steps inside with Tash. Principal Raza and Ernie follow.

My mom hugs me. "I had no idea what happened to you. I called the school, and nobody knew where you were. Tash thought you might be here."

"Hi, Noah," Tash says. "I'm sorry for what I did. You're probably thinking that the only reason I was hanging out with you is that I felt bad for you. And that was true, at first. Then I realized how much I love hanging out with you."

I don't say anything.

"Tash will put an end to those rumors. I have already sent an email to members of the school board clarifying the situation at your old school. I can't guarantee that your expulsion will go off the record. But I will do everything in my power to make sure that you don't have the same experience at my school," says Principal Raza.

"And I'll make some kick-ass food every time you come over. Which, from how much Tash talks about you, I think will be a lot," says Ernie.

I can't help but smile.

"Can you forgive me, Noah?" Tash asks.

"Of course I can," I say.

Tash hugs me, and I feel as though I'm exactly where I need to be.

Later that night, we all go to Tash's place for dinner. We talk, and we laugh. We share stories about the times we felt like outcasts. And of course, we talk about the mural.

Two robots surrounded by trash. The garbage covers most of the chaotic beauty that Tash created. The robots are holding nothing, because there's nothing left worth holding. They aren't sad. They aren't mad. Unlike humans, they don't get to feel anything.

I now realize that we're lucky to feel emotions. I know that I will still get angry at times, but that's okay. I know what to do now.

I know that I have the choice to create. My anger's in my art, and that's where it will stay.

About The Author

Nolan Janssens was born in Santiago, Chile, took his first steps in Antwerp, Belgium, and grew up in British Columbia, Canada. He was born without borders. Thinking outside the box is part of his make-up.

Nolan often subverts and challenges the status quo with humor, metaphor, and an eclectic mix of narratives. He graduated with honors from the Writing for Film & Television Program at Vancouver Film School in 2011 and is now pursuing his English degree at the University of British Columbia. He has had several of his works published.

58

About The Publisher

Story Shares is a nonprofit focused on supporting the millions of teens and adults who struggle with reading by creating a new shelf in the library specifically for them. The ever-growing collection features content that is compelling and culturally relevant for teens and adults, yet still readable at a range of lower reading levels.

Story Shares generates content by engaging deeply with writers, bringing together a community to create this new kind of book. With more intriguing and approachable stories to choose from, the teens and adults who have fallen behind are improving their skills and beginning to discover the joy of reading. For more information, visit storyshares.org.

Easy to Read. Hard to Put Down.

Made in the USA
Middletown, DE
20 January 2023